TERRIBLE TALES FROM SCHOOL

Kaye Umansky

Illustrated by **Tambe**

OXFORD

UNIVERSITY PRESS

Letter from the Author

I was born in 1946 – a year after World War Two ended. So I went to school in the 1950s. Schools were so different then. A lot stricter. Bullying was rife. Children were regularly punished, often for small misdemeanours. I can't say I have many happy memories. I am around the same age as Andrew's grandparents – Nan and Standad. The stories they tell are based on my own experiences.

My husband is twelve years older than me, and was evacuated during the war. He has a lot of unsettling stories to tell. Andrew's great-gran's unhappy account bears many similarities to them.

I enjoyed writing this story. I usually write fantasy stories, so it made a real change to write something based in real life – and to use personal experiences as a source for a work of fiction. I hope you enjoy it.

Kaye Umansky

Chapter 1
Nan's Tale

Do you notice something? Everybody's got a terrible tale from school. Adults, kids, even little tiddlers. Whatever their age, they can all trot out a long, rambling report of something truly awful that happened to them at school. They say things like 'I still have bad dreams' and 'I've never forgotten it' and 'It scarred me for life'. I only started thinking about this a few Sundays ago, when we were round at Nan and Standad's for lunch.

Nan and Standad are my mum's mum and dad, which makes them my grandparents. Nan's called Anne. Standad's called Stan. Standad is a sort of jokey name, and he likes it better than Grandad, because he used to play bass guitar in a band and doesn't think he's that old. (He is.) We go to them for lunch every Sunday, barring flood, fire, blizzards, alien invasion or particularly alarming viruses. It's a family tradition. Nan always does two huge roast chickens with allotment vegetables because there are *a lot* of us. (See what I did there? That's called a pun.)

I'm Andrew. I'm ten years old. I'm into science fiction. I've got a certificate for swimming ten lengths of the pool. I have a huge collection of novelty rubbers that I can't quite bring myself to throw away. I used to write stories (mostly about aliens) but don't so much these days.

My family consists of:

1. Me (Andrew)
2. Nan (Anne)

3. Standad (Stan)

4. Mum (Hannah)

5. Dad (Dan)

6. My little sister (Pansy)

7. Aunty Fran (Mum's sister)

8. Uncle Kev (her husband Kevin)

9. Their daughter Suzanne (my cousin)

Weirdly, almost all of our names have got *an* in. Only Uncle Kev doesn't follow the pattern, although he kind of does because his surname's McCann. Oh. Almost forgot.

10. Great-Gran.

Great-Gran is Nan's mum. She's about a thousand years old and lives with Nan and Standad except when they go on a cruise, when she comes to us. (She can't go to Aunty Fran's because they don't have a spare room.) She's got a bad leg and a hearing aid that gives out these tinny, high-pitched squeals because it's never tuned in right.

Here's a picture of our family tree.

FAMILY TREE

ME
Andrew

LITTLE SISTER
Pansy

COUSIN
Suzanne

DAD
Dan

MUM
Hannah

AUNTY
Fran

UNCLE
Kev

STANDAD
Stan

NAN
Anne

GREAT GRAN

So that's the ten of us. That's a *lot* of roast potatoes.

We were all squeezed round the kitchen table, using a strange assortment of living room chairs, kitchen chairs, garden chairs, stools and a low, canvas fold-up thing used for camping, which means that your nose is level with the table, even with two cushions. Suzanne and I always fight not to sit on that. I always lose because she cares more and shouts louder.

So. All of us were round the table except Great-Gran, who has her meals on a tray in an armchair in the corner because of her gammy leg.

'Here we are, Mum,' said Nan, plonking the tray down. 'I've cut it up small. Sit up a bit, or you'll spill it.'

'What is it?' asked Great-Gran, all suspicious, like she'd been given a plate of shredded car tyre. 'Not that patsy is it?' (She means pasta.)

'A nice bit of roast chicken. Put on your glasses – then you'll see.'

'Oooh, is it chicken? Lovely!'

She sounded surprised, although it's always roast chicken on Sundays.

'Who's for a leg?' asked Standad, who was doing the carving. I don't know why he bothers asking. We have exactly the same every week.

Finally we all had the correct bits on our plates, and started helping ourselves to vegetables. All except Suzanne, who was secretly texting under the table. (I don't mean *she* was

8

under the table. I mean she had her phone under the edge of the tablecloth.)

'Put that away, Suzanne,' said Aunty Fran. 'Not at the table. I've told you before.'

'Just a *minute*,' said Suzanne, in that whiny voice she's adopted ever since she started being best friends with Sophie Endersby, who's twelve and allowed to wear lipstick. (They stand in the street twirling their hair and talking loudly on their mobiles.) 'This is *important*.'

'Not so important it can't wait. Tell her, Kevin.'

'Put it away! You heard your mum,' said Uncle Kev automatically, helping himself to a mighty portion of potatoes.

Suzanne tossed her hair, shoved the phone in her pocket and jabbed crossly at a bit of broccoli.

'We never had mobile phones in my day,' said Nan. 'They weren't invented back in the fifties. We had to run to the chemist.'

'Why?' I piped up, from my gnome's camping stool. I didn't see why not having a futuristic phone would involve a trip to the chemist. It's hardly a medical emergency.

'He was the only one in the village who had a phone,' explained Nan. 'Mr Retalick, he was called. His wife bred Persian cats. One of them only had three legs. Everyone used his phone in an emergency.'

'Wasn't there a public call box?' asked Uncle Kev, taking another Yorkshire pudding. (Some people don't have Yorkshire pudding with chicken, but we do. Uncle Kev has more than most.)

'Yes, but the payphone was always out of order,' said Nan. 'The boys used to jam bottle caps in the slot. There was a lot of delinquency, back in those days. It's bad now, but back then, nothing was safe. Phone boxes were a real target. Good thing Mr Retalick had a phone, or I'd have lost my eye.'

This conversation was getting weirder by the minute.

'Why would you have lost your eye, Mum?' enquired my mum.

'Haven't I ever told you the story? I'm sure I have.'

Everyone assured her she hadn't.

'Well,' said Nan, 'a terrible thing happened to me at school, when I was nearly seven. I remember because it was coming up to my birthday. I sat next to this boy called Peter Kernahan. We weren't allowed to sit where we liked – the teacher chose. Boy, girl, boy, girl it went, in rows. Actually, Peter was all right. Had trouble reading, so I helped him. He was funny, though. A bit of a comedian. Used to hold belching contests at playtime. Only the boys joined in. Always wore a green jumper with a big hole in the sleeve. Summer, winter, always the same jumper. I don't know when it got washed.'

'When he was in bed?' I suggested.

'No. They'd never have got it washed and dried overnight. There weren't washing machines back then. Just soap and a mangle, wasn't it, Mum?'

'Eh?' said Great-Gran.

'You did the washing with soap and a mangle.'

'Hang on, dear, I'll turn this up.' Great-Gran fiddled with her hearing aid, which gave out fearsome howls. 'What?' she said.

'You washed the clothes with soap and a mangle. When I was little.'

'That's right,' said Great-Gran. 'I did. Getting them dry was the problem.'

'What's a mangle?' Pansy wanted to know.

'Two big rollers you fed the clothes through,' said Standad. 'You turned a handle and they revolved and squeezed the water out.'

'Where did the water go?'

'Into a bucket.'

'We kept ours in the garage,' said Nan. 'The water went straight down the drain. Didn't need a bucket.'

'Go on about Peter Kernahan, Mum,' said Aunty Fran. 'What's his manky jumper got to do with you nearly losing your eye?'

'Nothing to do with his jumper,' said Nan. 'He gave out the milk.'

'What milk?' I asked.

'We all got free milk at playtime in those days,' said Nan. 'It came in little bottles – you don't see them now, do you, Mum?'

'Eh?' said Great-Gran.

'Remember those little milk bottles we had at school? You don't see them now.'

'No,' agreed Great-Gran, a squeaky little mice chorus coming out of her ears. She popped a shaky spoonful of peas into her mouth. 'You don't.'

'Anyway, Peter was milk monitor,' went on Nan. 'He dropped a bottle on the radiator and it smashed into smithereens and a piece of glass shot out and went in my eye. The school had to run to Mr Retalick's and he called the doctor.'

'What – the whole school?' I asked, imagining hundreds of kids galloping wild-eyed down the road, clutching their dinky little milk bottles.

'Don't be so daft, Andrew,' said Dad, through a mouthful of spuds.

'Surely the school had a phone, Mum,' said Mum.

(There are so many mums in this story. I know it's confusing.)

'Ah. It did,' said Nan. 'But it was locked away in the headmaster's office. He was late in, see, because his car wouldn't start. Mr Fittock, he was called. Had one leg shorter than the other. Walked with a stick.'

'Didn't the caretaker have a key?' asked Mum.

'Nobody could find him. Mr Todd, he was called. He was at the vet's, you see. Emergency.

His dog had choked on a bone. Remember the caretaker's dog, Mum? The one that choked on the bone?'

No reply from Great-Gran's chair. Even her hearing aid had gone quiet.

'Joker, he was called,' Nan told us.

'*Choker* would have been better,' I said hilariously. Everyone ignored me.

'Did your eye hurt, Nanny?' asked Pansy, her eyes all big and round and caring.

'Hurt? I'll say it did. I wore a bandage for weeks, I know that.'

'Like my lip,' said Pansy. She gave a little pout. 'That hurt *bad*.'

Notice how she did that? Diverting someone else's pain to describe her own? While acting all babyish because she knows it gets attention?

To be fair, though, it was a bad accident. It happened when Pansy was in Reception. A boy called Christopher Logan pushed her off a chair and she bit through her bottom lip. She spent hours in Accident and Emergency. It happened two years ago and she still milks it for all it's worth. Well, it was a milk tooth (joke). Mind you, I'd probably milk it too, if it had happened to me.

'Poor old Pansy,' said Mum. 'That was horrible, wasn't it?'

'Yeth,' said Pansy, jutting out her lower lip. 'It wath Chwithtopher'th fault. He wathn't thowwy.'

Uh-oh. Pouting, lisping *and* dropping her r's. My sister was regressing to babyhood before my very eyes.

'Oh, I'm sure he was,' said Mum, falling for it as always.

'He wathn't.'

'He was, love. His mummy told me he was.'

'He wathn't. He laughed when the blood came out.'

'I'll tell you what *really* hurts,' said Standad darkly. 'A ruler on the knuckles. Now, *that* hurts.'

We all perked up, interested. We'd all had enough of Pan's lip, which she was always going on about. This was something new.

'Get the ruler, did you, Dad?' asked my Aunty Fran. 'You never told us that.'

'Oh yes,' said Standad. 'Happened a lot, back in those days. School was different then. A lot stricter. You kids don't know how lucky you are. See how we're all having a nice, sociable time over lunch? You couldn't do that, not back then. You weren't allowed to talk while you were eating. They made you finish everything on the plate, even if you hated it.'

'Same as my school,' agreed Nan. 'I still remember trying to get that cabbage down.'

'Did you have to eat gruel, Standad? Like Oliver Twist?' asked Pansy, thankfully dropping the baby stuff and returning to her actual age. She hasn't read the book, of course, but she's seen some of the musical on DVD.

Everybody smirked a bit. Standad's sensitive about his age.

'Hey, hey! I'm not *that* old.' He put down his knife and fork with a clatter, slightly miffed like we knew he would be. 'We're not talking Dickens here.'

'What did you get the ruler for?' asked Suzanne.

I was amazed she actually asked a question. Normally, she's only interested in celebrities.

'You won't believe it,' said Standad.

'What?' we all said, on tenterhooks.

'Whispering,' said Standad. He sat back in triumph, waiting for the reaction.

Chapter 2
More Tales

'Whispering?' we all shouted.

'Yep. Miss Goss, that was her name,' said Standad. 'She was standing on a ladder screwing in a light bulb, and her cardigan went up and I noticed the label on her woolly vest was sticking out. So I whispered to the girl sitting next to me – Maudie Johnson I think it was – I said, "Look, she's got her vest on inside out," and then Maudie got a fit of the giggles because I'd said a rude word.'

'What – *vest*?' said Aunty Fran, raising an eyebrow.

'Yep. Back then, no one talked about underwear, did they, Anne?'

'Nope,' agreed Nan. 'Not in public.'

'So old Goss heard,' continued Standad, 'and I got called out to the front of class and whacked across the knuckles.'

Everyone tutted and shook their heads in high disapproval at this barbaric punishment that was still allowed only sixty years ago.

Suzanne looked particularly horrified. She said, 'She was wearing a *woolly vest*?'

'Everyone wore vests back then,' said Nan. 'It was chilly. No central heating, was there, Stan?'

'Nope. Just a fire in the living room and maybe a one-bar electric fire in the bedroom before you went to bed. Just for an hour. If it was below freezing. We went to bed early with hot water bottles back then. No television to watch.'

'No television?' Pan's eyes nearly popped out of her head.

'Nope,' said Nan. 'No fridges or computers. We wore baggy navy gym shorts too. Well, the girls did. Big, thick, droopy ones. I remember when the elastic went on mine, right in the middle of Noah's Ark.'

'What?' we all said. This sounded interesting.

'Very painful, a whack across the knuckles,' said Standad, hoping to get more mileage from his ruler-on-the-knuckles story. But we had moved on and Nan and her baggy navy gym shorts had everyone's attention.

'We were doing a show of Noah's Ark,' said Nan. 'All the mums and dads were there, remember, Mum?'

'Eh?' said Great-Gran, suddenly waking up and staring down at her plate.

'Remember that time when I was a rabbit in Noah's Ark and came hopping down the aisle and my gym shorts fell down around my ankles? And the other rabbit went hopping on and left me behind? And both the giraffes fell over me and there was an animal pile-up and they had to stop the music?'

Great-Gran said, 'I've had to leave the Yorkshire pudding crust, Anne; it gets all under my dentures.'

'Leave it, then. Anyway, that's what happened and I never lived it down. I still blush to think of it now.'

Crikey. Nan had not one, but *two* terrible school stories. A nearly-lost eye and rogue baggy gym shorts. Hard to beat those.

Suzanne had her mobile out, and was texting again.

'Suzanne,' said Aunty Fran. 'What did I just say?'

'I'm just *trying* to get through to *Lizzie*,' whined Suzanne.

'I thought you didn't like Lizzie?'

'I *don't*. I want *Chantelle's* number, OK?'

'You're back friends with Chantelle again? I thought you two weren't speaking.'

'We're *not*. I left my pink *scarf* at her house. I want her to give it to *Rachel*.'

'You're back on speaking terms with Rachel?'

'Like, *yes*. She's only my *best friend*. After Sophie.'

'But you said you weren't going to her sleepover.'

'Only because *Georgia's* going. I said it had to be her or me. I'm not going to be in the same room as *her* after what she said about me last Wednesday. She's only going because Rachel's mum's, like, friends with Georgia's mum. She keeps showing off about it, but *I* don't care – I know Rachel hates her really.'

We were all stolidly eating through this, passing gravy and sprinkling salt and generally concentrating on the food. Nobody bothers to keep up with Suzanne's social life. She makes and breaks friends with all the girls in her class on an hourly basis. It's all about who's invited to sleepovers and parties and stuff. About how *Becky* went ice skating with *Shalimar* and didn't invite *Laura,* and *Emma* found out and told *Olivia* who's Laura's best friend and ... oh, I can't be bothered. You get the idea. Basically, her life is one long Greek tragedy. If you asked her for a bad school story, you'd be there all week.

'Girls,' said Mum, with a sigh. 'They can be very unkind. Remember Katy Coombes, Fran?'

'How could I forget?' said Aunty Fran, rolling her eyes. 'Pass the potatoes, would you, Dad? I'll just have a small one.'

Standad passed the potatoes via Uncle Kev, who grabbed another big one in passing.

'Who's Katy Coombes?' asked Pansy.

That caused the floodgates to open. Apparently, Mum and Aunty Fran had been at school with this girl called Katy Coombes, an almighty bully who pinched their playtime chocolate.

Chocolate? They were allowed to take *chocolate* to school? Things can't have been that bad in the old days, then. We're not allowed chocolate at our school. I was going to say so, but couldn't get a word in edgeways. I've never seen them so passionate.

According to them, this Katy Coombes had been a blight on their lives. If they didn't give up the chocolate, she would gang up on them in the girls' toilets with her horrible helpers, who were called Gillian Robinson and Lucy Dawes.

Honestly. All those years ago, and they still remembered the names. The saga went on and on. There was a lot more to it than chocolate stealing. There was name calling. Arm pinching. Hair pulling. Shoe throwing. Bag hiding. Spider-down-the-neck-of-the-dress action. All instigated by Katy Coombes, direct descendant of the Sheriff of Nottingham.

'I don't know about you, Han, but it genuinely scarred me for life,' said Aunty Fran, when they finally ran out of outrage. 'I still have dreams about it.'

'Absolutely,' agreed Mum. 'At least they have a proper bullying policy in schools these days. She'd never get away with it now.'

'She might,' said Suzanne. 'Olivia does. Do you know what she did? She—'

'I don't know what I'd do if I bumped into Katy Coombes in the supermarket,' went on Mum, not listening, still lost in the land of bitter memories. 'I really think I'd have to say something. I mean, she ought to know how hateful she was when she was a kid. Maybe she'd feel sorry.'

'I doubt it,' said Aunty Fran. 'Not her.'

'You're right, she wouldn't. Still. It'd make *me* feel better. I'd walk up to her and politely inform her that she totally ruined my schooldays. They're supposed to be the best days of your life, aren't they?'

'They weren't mine,' said Uncle Kev suddenly. He hadn't said a word up to now because he's a keen eater. But he had spotted a place to slip in and went for it. 'I still remember what happened in the changing room after we played Lipton Scouts.'

'What happened?' we asked.

'Got my nose broken,' said Uncle Kev. Mournfully, he fingered his nose, which does indeed have a funny lump in the middle.

'How?' we asked.

'The whole team jumped on me. Scragging, they called it. I ended up bashing my nose on the radiator.'

'Why?' asked Suzanne – a bit sneery because showing interest in your dad isn't cool. 'Why did they, like, *scrag* you?'

'We lost fourteen–nil. I was goalie. They took football seriously in my school.'

'I liked football,' said Dad, smoothly taking the conversational ball and running with it. Well, it was only fair. He hadn't said anything for ages. Not since telling me not to be daft, when I was making a joke about the fifties, involving milk and telephones. Even so, he deserved his turn. 'Played every week in the team. Always enjoyed it. Except for the time we played away and the coach went off the road.'

'Really?' said Mum. 'You've never told me that. What happened?'

'Well, it was a snowy day, see, and … '

Hey ho! We were off on a grim story involving a blizzard, a skid, a shattered windscreen (the coach's), a fractured arm (the driver's) and a broken leg (Dad's).

'I think the plaster cast's still up in the loft somewhere,' said Dad. (It is. I've seen it.)

'Uggh,' said Suzanne, with a theatrical little shudder. 'Creepy.'

'Why?' said Dad. 'It's a memento. All my mates signed it.'

I agreed with Suzanne, actually. It seems a weird thing to hang on to for thirty odd years.

At this point, we'd all finished, even Uncle Kev, and Nan began to clear the plates away.

'Everyone for apple pie?' she asked, cheerfully. Everyone was, apart from Great-Gran, who had dozed off again.

I love Nan's apple pie. I was just about to take the first bite, when Standad turned to me and said, 'So. How's school going with you these days, Andrew?'

Everyone looked at me expectantly.

'All right,' I said. 'Just – fine.'

There was a pause, then everyone went back to eating. Nan started talking about some television programme, and the conversation took a different turn.

I have to say it was an anticlimax. Everyone in the family had at least one hair-raising story of school horror. Everyone except me. And Great-Gran, I supposed. If she ever had one, she'd probably forgotten it.

The truth is, I liked school. Always had. I was no genius, but I did OK. The lessons could be a bit boring from time to time, but I usually managed to keep up and get my homework done, more or less. I'd never been in a fight. I had mates. No one picked on me. I was all right at sport – nothing spectacular, just all right. I got on OK with the teachers. I remembered my lines when I was in the school play.

Nope. Nothing bad had ever happened to me on school premises. Unless you count the time I forgot my packed lunch, but Dean Cooper shared his sandwiches with me so that didn't really count.

Later, after we'd all helped clear the table, and had a last cup of tea and bit of cake, we went home. When the weather's nice, we walk to Nan and Standad's, but that day it was raining buckets so we had the car. The awful anecdotes kept coming all the way home. Mum and Dad were on a roll and Pansy wasn't about to let her tooth story die.

'Thee?' she said, looking at her lip in the little mirror she keeps in her backpack. 'That'th where it happened, you can thtill thee the mark. Look, Andrew. Thee?'

'Mmm,' I said, looking out of the window, determined not to encourage her.

'Chrithtopher laughed. When the blood came out.'

'Yes, you said. Hey, look at that weird house – it's painted pink. Who'd paint their house pink? See that house, Mum?'

'It's funny what you said about breaking your leg on the bus, Dan,' said Mum, ignoring the pink house. 'Because it reminded me of the time when Katy Coombes tripped me up in PE … '

Off she went again. Dad countered with another horror story about the time someone hid his trousers and he had to walk home in his football shorts in the snow. It always seemed to be snowing in Dad's stories.

I kept quiet. I had nothing to say. We got home, I did my homework, played a couple of games online and took my boring, humdrum self off to bed.

37

Chapter 3
Yet More

The next day was Monday. I called for Dean, then we called for Khalif, who lives in the next street. We always walk to school together. Kirsty Stewart and Gemma Dickenson caught us up. They were going on about some Saturday-night talent show. I wasn't listening. I had something on my mind.

'What's the worst thing that's ever happened to you at school?' I said, when there was a lull in the conversation.

'What?' said Khalif.

'You know. Your worst ever day.'

'You are *kidding*, man?' said Dean. 'You were *there* when I had The Accident With My Head.'

Oh yes. Come to think of it, I was. Dean had fallen over a waste-paper basket and bashed his head on a window. He'd been taken away in an ambulance. He'd had several stitches.

'Yes,' I said, 'well, obviously, yes, that was bad. But at least you missed the spelling test.'

'Thanks for that,' said Dean, not laughing. 'Glad you think it's funny. Seeing as I'll have a scar for the rest of my life.'

'You can't see it, though,' I pointed out. 'It's under your hair.'

'And suppose I want to shave my head? What then?'

I didn't bother replying to this. Dean has longish, wavy, yellow hair cut in that style the girls seem to like. Mums call him 'that boy with the lovely hair'. He will *never* shave his head.

'My worst ever day was the first day I arrived, in Year Three,' said Khalif suddenly. 'Nobody spoke to me.'

'Only because you were the new boy and we didn't *know* you,' I said, rather guiltily. I remembered him sitting in a corner of the playground, all on his own, watching us enjoy a vigorous game of footie. 'Not because we didn't *like* you.'

'Still,' said Khalif. A little silence fell.

'We like you now,' said Gemma.

More awkward silence. I wished I hadn't brought the subject up.

'I know mine,' said Kirsty. 'It was when I fell off the bench in the concert in Year Two.'

I'd forgotten that.

It was the winter concert, and the choir, all dressed up as angels, were standing on benches, about to burst into song. Mrs Bunt struck up the starting chords on the piano and for some reason Kirsty lost her balance and fell sideways, knocking over the next kid, who fell into the next kid – basically the entire angelic host keeled over like skittles. They all wore wire wings which got tangled up. Heads were bumped, someone skinned their knee and started crying – it was chaos. Quite funny, though.

'*My* worst day was in Reception when I let the rabbit escape and it hid in the hedge and didn't get found for days and caught a cold and had to go to the vet's and have an injection,' said Gemma. 'Everyone blamed me.'

'Well, it was your fault,' I said. Well, it was. She wasn't supposed to take it out of the hutch without permission, let alone take it for a walk in the playground. We all told her it was her fault at the time and it remains the truth to this day.

'So what's yours, then?' snapped Gemma. All four of them stared at me.

'I don't have one,' I confessed.

'What d'you mean, you don't have one?'

'I just don't have one.'

We walked on. Dean, Khalif, Kirsty and Gemma continued droning on endlessly about the same dreary old traumatic stories.

I could contribute nothing. I trailed along behind, feeling excluded, like they were in some sort of survivors' club. I was just some dull, plodding kid who had never lived life on the edge and would have nothing of interest to tell his grandkids. It seemed like, compared to the rest of the world, my schooldays were incredibly boring.

In nursery, when the overhead skylight fell in, hurting no one but providing huge excitement, I was off school with earache.

When the games shed caught fire and the fire engine actually came into the playground, I was again off school. The dentist, that time.

I was fast giving up hope of ever being in the centre of any kind of drama.

* * *

School was uneventful that day, same as all the other days. I worked, I played, I had lunch. I painted a not-too-good picture of Henry VIII. There was some sort of competition our school was entering. The winner would win a thousand pounds' worth of books for their school. You could either write a story or do a painting about history, something like that. I wasn't that interested. I'm not the sort of person whose work gets chosen for competitions. I looked at my feeble effort and knew right away that it didn't stand a chance.

When home time came, I lingered behind to help Mrs Wilkinson finish washing up the paint jars. I like Mrs Wilkinson. She's tall and jolly and does art with us. She told me my Henry painting had a 'certain vigour' although we both knew it was rubbish.

'Mrs Wilkinson?' I said.

'Yes, Andrew?'

'Did anything really bad or funny ever happen to you at school?'

'What an odd thing to ask! What brought that on?'

'Nothing. I was just wondering.'

'Well, as a matter of fact, funny you should ask, I *did* have a rather upsetting experience. I don't think about it much, but last night I was watching a hockey match on television and it all came flooding back. I'd just started at secondary school and was trying to find my feet. There was this girl called Elizabeth Farrell – her mother was a teacher who actually taught our class so she was always chosen to fetch the register and run messages, which wasn't fair.'

'Did you *want* to fetch the register and run messages?' I enquired.

'Well, yes. It got you out of the classroom – broke up the routine a bit. Anyway, I never did get on with Elizabeth, but nothing prepared me for the time she ... '

And off she went on this endless tale about some girl she knew when she was eleven who had falsely accused her (Mrs Wilkinson) of stealing her (Elizabeth Farrell's) hockey stick. Both sticks looked similar, apparently. Both sets of parents were called in to the school to try and sort it out. (Well, being a teacher, Elizabeth Farrell's mum was there already.) For some reason, the dads took an instant dislike to each other. To cut a long story short, both of them lost it and there was an embarrassing tussle in the playground, made worse by the fact that Mrs Wilkinson's dad was the local doctor and supposed never to do any harm. The hockey stick was never found. Everyone took Elizabeth Farrell's side, with her mum being a teacher and all, and whispered about Mrs Wilkinson behind her back.

Needless to say, the incident scarred her for life.

On the way home, I called in at the corner shop. The owner is a nice, quiet man called Mr Jakes, who came to live in England after college and told me stories sometimes about his childhood.

I bought some raisins and a packet of cheese and onion crisps. While I was waiting for my change, I said, 'What was your school like when you were a kid, Mr Jakes?'

'It had a tin roof,' said Mr Jakes. 'Too hot in the summer, freezing in winter. When I was about your age, it got swept away by an avalanche. Seven pence change. Do you want a bag?'

Chapter 4
Great-Gran's Tale

After school on Wednesdays, I go to Nan and Standad's for tea. This is because Mum takes Pansy to her dancing class and Dad doesn't get home till seven. I like it, actually. They get in my favourite biscuits and there's always cake and ice cream and they cut the crusts off the sandwiches.

I have to admit that they spoil me a bit. Pansy usually gets most of the attention, but Wednesday nights are all about me. I just plonk myself next to Great-Gran on the sofa in the living room and we watch telly while Nan and Standad run about the kitchen doing things for us. Great-Gran doesn't care what we watch, so I have complete charge of the remote, which doesn't happen at home. She snoozes and I channel-hop like crazy.

This particular Wednesday, nobody answered when I rang the doorbell. I guessed they were up at the allotment and had forgotten the time because they were enjoying themselves so much. I don't get why old people like gardening. They always spend hours groaning and clutching at their backs afterwards. Where's the fun in that?

I knew Great-Gran would be in the kitchen in her armchair, probably with her hearing aid turned off. I knew the drill.

I walked round to the side and hammered on the kitchen window.

'Gran!' I bellowed. 'It's Andrew! Let me in!'

'Who?' quavered Great-Gran's old voice.

'Me! Andrew! I've come for tea! Let me in!'

'Andrew? Is that you?'

'Yes! Let me in, will you?'

'Coming right away, lovey,' called Great-Gran. Which wasn't that accurate, because it took her forever to get out of her chair, find her stick, adjust her many shawls and cardigans and shuffle round to the front door. That's hardly

right away, is it? Before the ice caps melt would
be more accurate.

When she finally let me in, I gave her the usual dutiful peck, then went into the kitchen to help myself to orange juice. She shuffled along behind and stood beaming at me from the kitchen doorway. She had her hearing aid in and seemed quite sprightly. One of her good days.

'They've changed my tablets,' she announced. 'My knee's feeling a lot better.'

'Great!' I said. 'Is your hearing aid tuned in properly?'

'It is. New batteries. Mind you, it's not so much the batteries that give me trouble. It's when everyone talks at once and I can't see their lips. I'm better when it's just one or two people.'

'Oh. Right,' I said. I hadn't realized that. 'So. Shall we have a cup of tea?'

'Let's,' said Great-Gran. She gave a conspiratorial little wink. 'If we have it now, I'll give myself an extra couple of sugars. Don't let Anne know though; she says it's bad for me.

I'll make it, lovey. You go and watch your programmes.'

'In a bit,' I said. 'Better do my homework first.'

It was History and we were doing World War Two. I had to write a story about being evacuated. I didn't think it would take long. I've seen *Bedknobs and Broomsticks*. That's a film set during the war. I could dash something off in no time.

Great-Gran pottered about slowly with mugs and milk and the kettle while I sat down at the kitchen table and got out my writing book and pencil case. I turned to a fresh page and took up the pencil.

'Have a biscuit, sweetheart,' said Great-Gran, rattling the tin under my nose. 'Good for the brains.'

'Thanks.' I helped myself to a digestive. She continued to shake, so I took a second. And a figgy roll, just because it looked sad on its own and might possibly count towards my five-a-day.

'What are you doing, anyway? Sums, is it?'

'No. I'm writing about being evacuated during the war. You know? When all the little kids got put on trains and sent away to the country to avoid the bombs?'

'Yes,' said Great-Gran, shakily pouring milk into a mug. 'I know. I was one of 'em.'

'Were you?' I looked up, startled.

Was she? Well, come to think of it, it made sense. She's in her eighties now, so she would have been a little kid back in 1939, when the war started.

How weird. I never thought of that when we were doing the war in school. It seemed unreal, like some made-up long-ago story. But, of course, it was real. And my great-gran was part of it.

'So – you actually went on one of those trains?' I asked.

'I did. Me and George.'

'Who?'

'George, my little brother.'

Great-Gran had a brother called George?
I didn't know that. I opened my mouth,
ready to ask about him, then shut it again.
If George never showed up at the Sunday
lunches and nobody ever mentioned him,
the chances were he was – well – dead. Either
that, or he was the villain of the family who
ran away with the ancestral silver. Of the two
possibilities, death seemed more likely.

'What was it like?' I asked. 'Being an
evacuee?'

'Horrible,' said Great-Gran. 'I missed my
mum something rotten. But I tried not to
show it because of George. I had to look
after him, see. He was only four. Just a baby,
really.'

'How old were you?' I asked.

'Six.'

Six! The same age as Pansy. I tried to
imagine sending my little sister off on a train
to live with total strangers. Wearing weird,
old-fashioned clothes and carrying a gas

mask and a little suitcase. With the added responsibility of looking after an even younger brother.

I couldn't do it. Pan tried a sleepover at her best friend's house and wept so bitterly the second the light went out that Dad had to go and fetch her. As for responsibility – well, let's just say that the goldfish she begged for and promised to feed regularly was very short-lived. As a child, Great-Gran had clearly been made of sterner stuff. But then, there was a war on. She didn't have a choice.

Neither did poor little George, of course. Whatever did a four-year-old make of it all? Things blowing up and sirens and gas masks and having to leave your mum?

'Who did you live with, Gran?' I asked.

'Different families. We got moved around a lot. Some were quite kind. Some weren't. One lot ate in the dining room and made George and me eat with the maid in the kitchen. They had a little girl about my age, but we weren't allowed to touch her toys. The best one was a farm down in Dorset. We learned how to milk the cows. Our job was to collect the eggs in the morning before walking the three miles to school.'

Three *miles*? That's a long way for a couple of little kids.

'What was the school like?' I asked. After walking three miles to get there, I hoped it was a good one.

'Much like the others. We went to four altogether, I think. Or maybe five. Hated all of 'em, I know that.'

'Why?'

'Desks in rows. Bolted down, they were, with attached seats. You had to watch out for splinters. The boilers never worked right, so we were always cold. Outside toilets. Got shouted at by the teachers a lot. Spent most of our time just copying stuff down. A lot of nastiness in the playground. The local village kids didn't like us evacuees. Said we came from the slums. Made out we smelled. Said we talked funny. Georgie had a stone thrown at him – cut him on the ear. I saw to the boy that threw it, mind.'

'How?' I asked.

'Never you mind,' said Great-Gran darkly. 'He didn't throw another, I'll tell you that. Here's your tea, sweetheart.'

I jumped up hastily and took the mug out of her shaky old hand before it slopped.

'Sit down,' I said. 'Tell me more.'

Did I say earlier on that if Great-Gran had a terrible school story, she had probably forgotten it? I was wrong. She did, and she hadn't. In fact, I'd never heard her talk so much.

It was really, really interesting.

A bit later, Nan and Standad arrived back with a load of shopping. Great-Gran was telling me about all these illnesses that kids got back then. Whooping cough. Polio. Mumps.

Both she and George got through the war and eventually went back home to live with their parents. That lasted for a year.

George died of scarlet fever, aged nine.

Nan and Standad were listening while they quietly put away the shopping.

'We've got a picture of him, haven't we?' said Nan gently. 'Little George. You and him together. In the old box in the sideboard, I think.'

'I know where it is,' said Standad. 'I'll find it. Mum, why don't you and Andrew take your tea and sit on the sofa and stick on the TV while we get some food organized?'

So that's what we did, my great-gran and I. We sat on the sofa with our tea – but we didn't switch on the television. Instead, we looked through a box of weird old black-and-white photographs that I never knew existed.

There were tiny little snaps of various young men standing proudly next to vintage motor cars and ladies in flowery dresses posing in gardens. There were lots of old men with whiskers and lots of fearsome-looking old women with hatchet faces. Some of them Great-Gran knew – a cousin here, an uncle there – others she didn't.

There were some pointless photos of the featureless seaside, taken from miles away, just cliffs and sand and water that could have been Southend, Honolulu or Mars.

There were a couple of photos of Great-Gran as a young woman. She was quite pretty despite the weird hairstyle.

And right at the bottom, there was a tiny square one of two small children standing hand in hand under a tree. You couldn't see them too well: the photo was faded and quite badly creased.

'That's us,' said Great-Gran. 'Me and George. Just before they sent us away.'

I studied the picture.

'What was your name, Gran?' I asked.

'Same one I've got today. Janet. No one left to call me it now.'

That seems sad, somehow. Getting so old that no one calls you by your name. I didn't know what to say.

I was glad when Nan gave us a shout that tea was ready and Standad came to help Great-Gran off the sofa and back into the kitchen. It was

vegetable soup and cheese toasties. My favourite.

Dad came to pick me up as usual. We got home just after seven and I borrowed Mum's laptop and went straight up to my room to do my homework.

It took longer than usual.

Chapter 5
Water

School always starts with assembly. Our head teacher, Mrs Sugden, reads out any notices about what's happening and presents any prizes or awards that are going and then gives a pep talk – an encouraging little speech about doing your best and always being helpful and not dropping litter or running in the corridors. Sometimes, some kid stands up and reads out a poem or a book review. Sometimes a group enacts a short play, which often isn't great in my opinion. Particularly good pieces of art are held up to be admired. Then we sing a song and go back to class. When I was younger, I regularly stood up and read out stories I'd written. Not since I'd been in Year Six, though. I still liked reading, but I'd got out of the habit of writing for fun.

This particular morning, Mrs Sugden reminded the teachers that any late entries for

the history competition had to be handed in as they were due to be sent off that very day to be judged. She reminded everyone about netball practice after school. And she reminded the boys that the glorious new boys' toilets were now open and ready for use. We shouldn't use the old ones any more because shortly the builders would be coming in to rip out all the fixtures and fittings and turn the space into a lovely new library.

Our school is pretty ancient. They're always demolishing old bits and building on new bits to drag us into the twenty-first century. It's an ongoing project.

This was good news in one way, because the old toilets were hardly the vision of gleaming porcelain, hygienic soap dispensers and flattering mirrors that the new ones would doubtlessly be. The loos didn't flush well, the sinks were cracked and all but one of the hot taps didn't work. On the other hand, they were conveniently situated just along the corridor from our Year Six classroom, whereas the new ones were right at the other end of the school.

Anyway. That was the toilet news. There wasn't much else of interest, except that a local children's author was coming in to talk to Year

Two about her new book and we were all to be on our best behaviour when moving about the corridors. Her name was Tamara Brook-Sweeting. Her book would be on sale in the library at lunch hour for anyone who had brought some money. (I hadn't.)

We went back to class and got out our Maths books while Khalif collected up our homework and handed it in to Mr Joshy, our teacher.

He's nice, Mr Joshy. He cracks a lot of jokes. He tells us that if we don't behave, he'll leave the teaching profession and follow his life's dream, which is to open a laundrette. He says he will call it Joshy's Flashy Wishy-Washy. And we'll be left without anyone to teach us and as a result will be hopeless failures in life and never win any money on TV quiz shows.

That morning, we did Maths, followed by quiet reading, while Mr Joshy glanced over our homework. The pile was going down quite quickly. He hadn't got to mine yet, I noticed.

I got through two chapters of *Treasure Island*.

At lunch, there was my least favourite pudding. It's some sort of lemon mousse and is incredibly sweet yet simultaneously so sharp it makes your eyes water. Dean isn't keen either. For some stupid reason he and I got into this water-drinking competition. It started off just taking the lemon taste away, then developed into a contest. After three beakers, we gave up. There's only so much water you can drink in one go, unless you've struggled in from the desert, in which case you might be able to manage four. Anyway, apparently it's dangerous to drink too much water.

(We, of course, got into the water after the *dessert*, not the desert. I'm not sure that's a great joke, but I'm putting it in anyway.)

I noticed the visiting children's author sitting on the teachers' table. She had big wooden earrings and frizzy hair. She wore a long brown skirt that dragged on the floor and weird sandals. The book she had written had a unicorn on the front and was called *In a Moonlit Forest*. I know that because I had noticed there was a sort of shrine to her in the entrance hall – a cloth-covered table with a vase of flowers and her photo and loads of copies of the book and WELCOME TAMARA BROOK-SWEETING written in huge letters.

The photo showed her quite a bit younger than she really was. She was eating a jacket potato and healthy salad with an apple for pudding, so was probably vegetarian. (Not in the photo, obviously. I mean for lunch.) She wasn't coming into our class. Year Six are too old for Moonlit Forests. I certainly know I'm way past unicorns.

In the afternoon, Dean and I put the finishing touches to our bug hotel, which we were making in Design and Technology. We named it Louse Vegas. I was halfway through gluing the sign on when I suddenly realized I needed the toilet. All that lunchtime water had finally filtered through.

'I wish I hadn't drunk all that water,' I said to Dean.

'You should have gone to the new toilets after lunch,' said Dean. 'I did.'

I asked Mr Joshy if I could be excused. He said that depended on what I'd done. I gave a feeble smile and said, 'Please, sir. I have to. It's essential.'

'Like following one's path in life, young Andrew,' said Mr Joshy. 'That's essential. I'm just about to read your History essay. If it's anything like your last effort, that – is – it. I give in. *Finito.* My teaching days are over. The laundrette beckons and I shall go.'

'Please, sir,' I begged, 'can we talk about it when I get back?'

'Oh, go on, then! Hurry it up.'

I have to say, I was desperate. I really should have asked before. I dashed from the classroom and scooted along the corridor, automatically braking as I reached the door of the old boys' toilets. I was just about to push it open when I was brought up short by the yellow tape stretched across the entrance.

Ah. Right. We weren't supposed to use it any more. It was out of bounds.

Of course, thinking I was almost there brought on the need to go *right away*. Now. *This instant.* No way could I go on the long trek to strange new toilets on the other side of the school. It would mean traversing three corridors. Not a chance.

I ducked under the yellow tape.

I'll spare you the details. All you need to know is that I did the necessary and the relief was immense. As always, the flush took a few goes before it worked. The chain's short and it needs a special knack.

I went to wash my hands, which were covered in toilet-chain rust and sticky with glue.

I don't know how old the plumbing was in these toilets. I would guess prehistoric. Hand washing was easier said than done, that's for sure. There were three old, cracked sinks. Two of the taps gave out a miserly trickle of cold water and two sinks were completely blocked, even with the plugs missing. It took all day for them to drain. The third had hot water and drained a bit better, but the tap was stiff. There was no soap.

Still. Any port in a storm, as Nan says.

I went for the one working hot tap. The stiff one. I tried to turn it. Nothing. I tried with both hands. Still nothing. It didn't help that my fingers were slippery with bug hotel glue. I took off a shoe and tried hammering it sideways. More nothing. That tap did not want to budge.

When Mum wants to get the top off a jam jar or something, and it's tight, she uses a tea towel to get a better grip. I didn't have a tea towel, so I used my sock. I peeled it off my right foot, wrapped it around my hand, grasped the tap, took a deep breath and tried one last time, bearing down and twisting with all my weight while standing on my other foot, carefully keeping the bare one off the grubby floor.

It worked! The tap suddenly gave way with a jerk and a raging spurt of warm water came gushing into the sink, splashing the front of my shirt and trousers and sending me off balance. The sock slithered into the sink, tugged downwards by the water. I staggered backwards with a yelp, arms wheeling. In doing so, I scraped my heel, which hurt like mad. Water splashed out. The sink was filling up really quickly because the plughole was suffering from sock blockage.

I had to turn the tap off. Dodging the splashing water, I approached from the side and got a grip on it. It just spun round uselessly while water continued to gush out like the Niagara Falls. Something very wrong there. Using the tips of my fingers, I gingerly fished my sock out of the sink, hoping that the draining-away process would begin. It didn't. Instead, the water rose and overflowed on to the floor. Some of it went into my shoe, which I hadn't yet had time to put back on, what with all the drama.

I had a last, despairing go at the tap, which twirled merrily around, clearly broken beyond repair. More water slopped out of the sink. There was already quite a big puddle.

I was panicking a bit. There was nothing else I could think of to do. The situation was clearly beyond me, so I had to get help. Race to the office, explain what was happening and ask them to fetch Alan the caretaker. That's what needed to be done. For a second,

I remembered Nan's eye story, where the caretaker's dog (Joker) had choked on a bone, thus preventing the caretaker from dealing with an emergency. Luckily, Alan doesn't have a dog.

The entire floor was awash now. It was like being in a paddling pool. My heel was still hurting, and the scrape was bleeding a bit. I wrung out my sock, snatched up my soaked shoe, splashed through the warm puddle that lay between me and the door, limped through the yellow tape and out into the corridor ...

... almost colliding with Mrs Sugden, who was in the process of showing the visiting author the delightful artwork displayed around the school. They were on the way to the library, I think, where she was doing her talk.

'Good gracious!' said Mrs Sugden. 'What's going on?'

'Accident!' I gabbled. 'The tap's broken. Can't stop the water!'

'So I see,' said Mrs Sugden, staring at my soaked front, my hand-held shoe and sock and my big, bare, bleeding foot. The puddle, moving at a fast, steady pace, had followed me out into the corridor and was spreading hugely by the second. It swirled around Tamara Brook-Sweeting's big sandals. Her trailing skirt was already soaking it up. She gave a little whimper and stepped quickly to one side.

'I'll run and tell Miss Joy, shall I?' I asked Mrs Sugden. 'She'll get Alan.'

'Yes,' said Mrs Sugden tightly. 'You do that. But please don't run. And dry your feet.' She turned to Tamara Brook-Sweeting. 'These things happen from time to time, I'm afraid. Old plumbing. We've actually just replaced these old toilets with new ones. I did announce it in assembly. Andrew clearly didn't hear, or notice the yellow tape. Oh *dear*, are your feet wet? I am *so* sorry. Now, moving on, as you see, Year Five have been painting in the style of Monet ...'

They stepped over the huge, rippling puddle and carried on down the corridor, Tamara Brook-Sweeting's skirt leaving a wet slug-trail behind.

I hobbled along to reception to deliver the bad news. To add to the horror of it all, when crossing the foyer, in my haste I accidentally banged into the author shrine. The vase of flowers tipped over and broke, spilling water on to the pile of brand-new books. That didn't go down at all well with Miss Joy, the school secretary. I think she had personally arranged the table.

Miss Joy listened to my garbled tale, picked up the phone to summon Alan, then carefully cleaned up the table and used her own box of tissues to blot all the damp copies of *In a Moonlit Forest*. I offered to help, but she declined and went off in search of a mop with a face like thunder. I mean Miss Joy's face was like thunder, not the mop's.

I must say it was a relief to hand over the responsibility of flood prevention to Alan and his trusty box of spanners. He's a caretaker, though, not a superhero, and by the time he got there most of the corridor was under water. To get back to my classroom, I actually took off the other sock and shoe, rolled up my trousers and paddled.

Then, of course, I had to face my classmates with a huge, wet stain across the front of my trousers. That caused a bit of mirth. A lot of comments like, 'Oh, he *says* it's water!' and so on. I tried to dry my sock on the radiator, but the girls complained. The wet shoe felt horrible – all cold and slimy.

Mr Joshy took pity on me, gave me a plaster for my heel and let me stay in at afternoon break. I sat in the empty classroom, hopelessly blotting myself with an old towel and wondering if I'd get into serious trouble for:

1. ignoring instructions
2. bypassing yellow tape
3. using out-of-date plumbing
4. breaking said out-of-date plumbing
5. smashing a vase
6. ruining a load of books
7. showing the school up in front of a visitor.

I didn't have long to wait. Mr Joshy came back just before the whistle and told me that Mrs Sugden wanted to see me.

I knocked on her office door, which was open. She was sitting at her desk, looking down at what transpired was my essay. I'd typed it up on Mum's computer. It was quite long.

'Come in, Andrew,' she said. 'Are you dry?'

'More or less,' I said.

'Then have a seat.'

I sat down and waited.

'Your essay,' she said, holding it up. '"George's Story". Mr Joshy handed it in. I've just read it.'

'Oh,' I said. 'Right.'

'You sound surprised.'

'I thought you were going to tell me off about the water.'

'Mmm. Did you write this yourself?'

'Yes,' I said. 'Of course.'

'No help at all?'

'No. Yes. I mean, I wrote it. But I got it all from my great-gran. She was an evacuee in the war.'

'Ah. So – she would be Janet in your story?'

'That's right. George was her little brother.'

'And you've told the story of their evacuation in his words.'

'Yes.'

'What made you do that? Use a four-year-old boy as a narrator?'

'I don't know. I suppose – well, I thought he had a story to tell. He died, you see, when he was younger than me. Before he got the chance to tell it. Was it a bad idea?'

'No,' said Mrs Sugden. 'It was a wonderful idea. You captured his voice perfectly. I don't mind telling you, it brought a lump to my throat. The opening paragraph is especially moving, when the two of them are leaving on the train and he sees their mother on the platform. And Janet gives him a sugar lump to stop him crying.'

'Well, that's what happened. I'm only saying what my great-gran told me.'

'Yes. But it's the way you say it. It sounds – well, very genuine. Very real.'

I didn't know what to say to that. I know I can write quite well when I can be bothered. These days, that's not so often. I'd forgotten what it felt like to be complimented.

'In fact,' went on Mrs Sugden, 'it's such a good piece of work that I'd like to submit it for the history competition. Would you have any objections?'

No. Obviously not.

'Well, congratulations, Andrew. It's a long time since we had anything this good from you. It's nice to know you're back on form. I'll make a copy for you before we send it off. Has your great-gran read it?'

'No, not yet.'

'Well, I think she'll feel you've done them both justice.' Mrs Sugden stood up. 'And now I must go and collect our author.'

I said, 'I'm sorry about knocking the flowers over and spoiling her books.'

'Ah, well. I shall just have to buy them for the library.'

'Sorry I broke the tap too.'

'Just pay attention in assembly in future, Andrew. The school has a responsibility to keep you all safe. The tape was there for a reason. Off you go then, back to class.'

And that was that.

Not such a terrible day after all.

Chapter 6
Lunch Again

I didn't win the history competition. It would have made a perfect ending, but I didn't. Some girl from another school wrote a thing from the point of view of Anne Boleyn, set in Henry VIII's palace. That got the first prize – the thousand pounds' worth of books. It was good, actually.

But guess what?

I CAME SECOND!

I could hardly believe it myself when Mrs Sugden told me. That means the school gets three hundred pounds' worth of books and a free visit from a children's author. I hope it's not Tamara Brook-Sweeting.

The ten finalists got their work displayed in the big town library. The mayor was there to hand out certificates. Mum, Dad, Nan, Standad and Pansy all came along and stood about looking proud when I got interviewed by a reporter called Sonia from the local paper. Great-Gran had a cold, so she couldn't come. When I explained to Sonia that it was all down to her (Great-Gran) that my essay came out the way it did, she suggested that she (Sonia) and a photographer come to Nan and Standad's to take a picture of us together.

Great-Gran said it was a load of old nonsense. What did they want a picture of her for? But I noticed that she wore her best cardigan and had her hair done for the occasion.

The photo appeared in the paper above a headline that read:

LOCAL BOY THANKS
GREAT-GRANDMOTHER
FOR HELPING HIM WIN
PRIZE FOR WAR STORY

It's not a great photo. Great-Gran's squinting and my hair's all weird. Nan loves it, though, and says she'll frame it. It will join the pantheon of favourite family photos displayed on the mantelpiece, along with Standad on his motorbike, Aunty Fran and Uncle Kev's wedding, Mum and Dad's wedding, Pansy posing in a tutu and Suzanne on a swing in the garden when she still knew how to smile.

I haven't told you what Great-Gran said about George's story when she first read it. Not much, actually. She just gave a little sigh, patted me on the knee and said, 'Yes, lovey. That was it.'

Nan and Mum were more emotional. They both snivelled quite a lot. So did Pansy when she understood what had happened to George in the end. She asked if she could have the little black-and-white picture of Janet and George and put it in her fairy treasure chest, where she keeps all her best things. Great-Gran said of course she could, so it's in our house now.

The next Sunday at the family gathering round the table, they made me read out George's story to Aunty Fran and Uncle Kev and Suzanne. A clap on the back from Uncle Kev and more tears from Aunty Fran. Suzanne didn't cry, but at least she had her mobile turned off and listened. And when we left that night, I noticed she gave Great-Gran an especially big hug.

So. Back to where we started. Terrible tales from school.

I still didn't really have one of my own. I mean, the plumbing disaster turned out to be not that big a deal. Everyone had stopped teasing me about my stain of shame by home time. My scraped heel healed (no scar). The sock, shoe and trousers dried out. The flood receded under Alan's formidable powers. There was, in fact, no real harm done, either to school property or myself. Although, along with three hundred pounds' worth of brand-new stock (thanks to me), the new library will have an awful lot of signed, water-stained books about unicorns. (Also thanks to me.)

I was resigned to never having a really good dramatic tale of my own to tell.

Then, two weeks ago, we went on a school trip to Cornwall and three of us got accidentally separated on a walk and the fog came down and Gemma fell in a ditch and twisted her ankle and

I tried giving her a piggyback and tripped over a log and twisted *my* ankle and ...

No. That's another story.